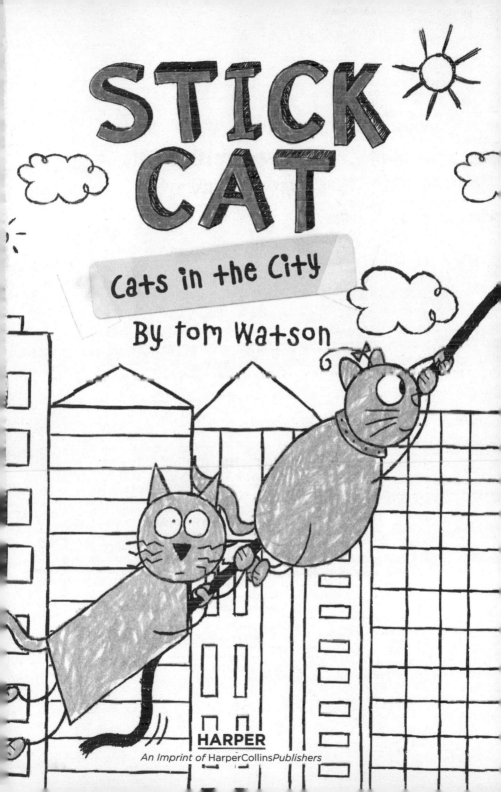

Dedicated to Elizabeth.
(YAt BY WITW ILY)

Stick Cat: Cats in the City
Copyright © 2017 by Tom Watson
Illustrations by Ethan Long based on original sketches by Tom Watson
All rights reserved. Printed in the United States of America.
No part of this book may be used or reproduced in any manner whatsoever without
written permission except in the case of brief quotations embodied in critical articles and reviews.
For information address HarperCollins Children's Books, a division of HarperCollins Publishers,
195 Broadway, New York, NY 10007.
www.harpercollinschildrens.com

Library of Congress Control Number: 2016957935
ISBN 978-0-06-241102-0

Typography by Jeff Shake
17 18 19 20 21 CG/LSCH 10 9 8 7 6 5 4 3 2 1
❖
First Edition

Table of Contents

Chapter 1(A)

WHAT? IT'S POSSIBLE.

I think she might like me. She liked my first Stick Cat story. She told me.

You know who I'm talking about, right?

Mary. The one I wrote Stick Cat for? She likes cats. She carries all her books in this big denim shoulder bag that has a cat face sewn onto it. She's got lots of stuff in that bag with her books. I've seen her pull out a hairbrush, a plastic container with a

sandwich in it, a little packet of tissues, a
long string of ponytail rubber band things,
and a soft, flimsy Frisbee, which she throws
at recess. There are probably another
dozen things in there too.

Why do girls carry so much stuff anyway?
I don't understand them.

Maybe there's a journal in there too. And
maybe Mary wrote all about reading the
first Stick Cat story. And maybe she wrote
about how she
liked it. And
maybe she wrote
about how she
likes me.

What? It's possible.

So, the thing is . . . umm, I lied.

But I didn't do it on purpose.

I really did *intend* to write just one Stick Cat story. But it turns out that Mary liked it. And since she liked it—and now says "Hi" to me—I thought it might be in my best interest to write another one, if you know what I mean.

What choice do I have? She might like me.

What? It's possible.

*Note to self: tear out these first couple of pages before letting Mary read the new Stick Cat story.

Chapter 1

MESMERIZED

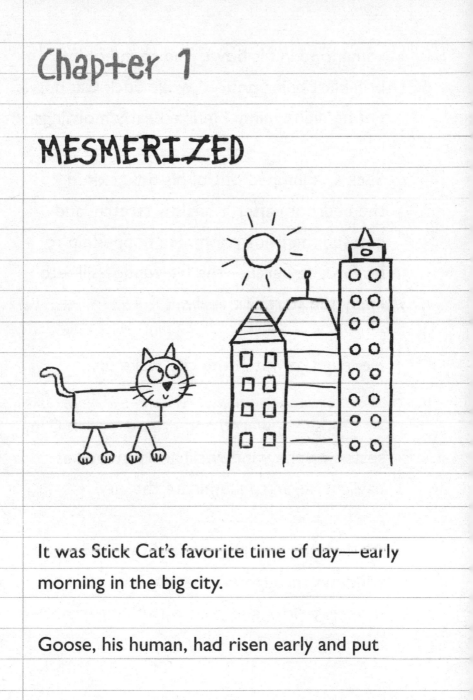

It was Stick Cat's favorite time of day—early morning in the big city.

Goose, his human, had risen early and put

some food in his bowl. The sound of his breakfast being poured woke Stick Cat up, but he didn't mind. He liked early mornings.

Stick Cat jumped out of his box, exited the bedroom after a healthy stretch, and crossed the living room. He hopped up to his favorite perch—the big windowsill—to enjoy the start of the day.

He loved to watch the city wake up.

As Goose showered and dressed, Stick Cat rested on the windowsill and watched as daylight began to illuminate the city.

As the sun rose, he watched thousands of windows throughout the city begin to glow orange, yellow, and gold with that early-morning light.

Goose approached him as Stick Cat stared
out the window.

"It's pretty, isn't it?" he said,
and scratched Stick Cat
behind the left ear. It was
one of his favorite places—
and Goose knew it. Stick
Cat turned his head and allowed Goose to
scratch behind his right ear too.

"See you tonight," Goose said. He patted his
pockets to ensure that he had his cell phone,
wallet, and keys. He did. And he left.

Stick Cat turned back to the window.

On these summer mornings, Stick Cat loved
to watch the building across the alley the
most. It's where Mr. Music tuned the pianos

in the old factory and played short concerts for Stick Cat. In the summer, that building would catch the very first daylight. But it was what happened next that always caught and kept Stick Cat's attention.

As the morning minutes passed, the sun rose slowly higher, and buildings off to Stick Cat's left began to cast shadows on Mr. Music's building. For several minutes, he watched as the shadow from one skyscraper's pole slid along the building. There was a flag atop that pole and, since it was a breezy morning, it flapped in the wind.

Stick Cat had seen it

before on many other summer mornings, but it remained fascinating to him.

Everything else moved so slowly, methodically, and deliberately, but the shadow from that flag flapped and shimmied. It made Stick Cat think that the morning was waving at him—welcoming him to the new day.

He watched it. And watched it. And watched it.

Mesmerized.

Until something startled him out of his trance.

"Stick Cat!"

It was Edith.

Chapter 2

AN INVITATION

Stick Cat smiled. He
couldn't help himself.
He knew exactly
what he would see
when he went into
the bathroom to
meet up with Edith. She would be stuck in
the wall between their apartments again.

The two of them had scratched and clawed
a hole in the wall at the back of their
respective bathroom cabinets. Edith climbed
through that wall almost every day to come
to Stick Cat's apartment.

They treasure hunted together, found things in Stick Cat's kitchen to snack on, or napped together on the windowsill. Sometimes, their days were far more exciting—like the time they rescued Mr. Music when his arms were trapped inside a grand piano across the alley.

Stick Cat wondered what this day would bring.

One thing he didn't wonder about was where he would find Edith. He was quite certain she would be stuck in the hole in the bathroom wall. It had been happening more and more lately. In fact, in the past couple of months, Stick Cat figured he must have yanked Edith out of her wedged position more than twenty times.

"Stick Cat!"

"I'm right here," he said upon entering the bathroom. "I'll pull you out in just a second."

"Pull me out of what?" Edith asked loudly.

"Out of the hole in the wall," he said, and opened the bathroom cabinet. "Just like I've done—"

But Stick Cat didn't finish his sentence.

That's because Edith wasn't stuck in the wall at all. She hadn't even started climbing through yet. She just stood on her side looking through the hole.

"Oh, I thought you were, umm . . . ," Stick Cat said, and stopped himself.

"You thought I was what?" Edith asked. She seemed offended.

"I thought you were, you know."

"What?"

"Umm," Stick Cat said, and began to slap gently at a loose edge of toilet paper on a spare roll in the cabinet. "Hey, look at this! This is really fun. Look how it flutters away and then settles back into its original position. Pretty neat, hunh?"

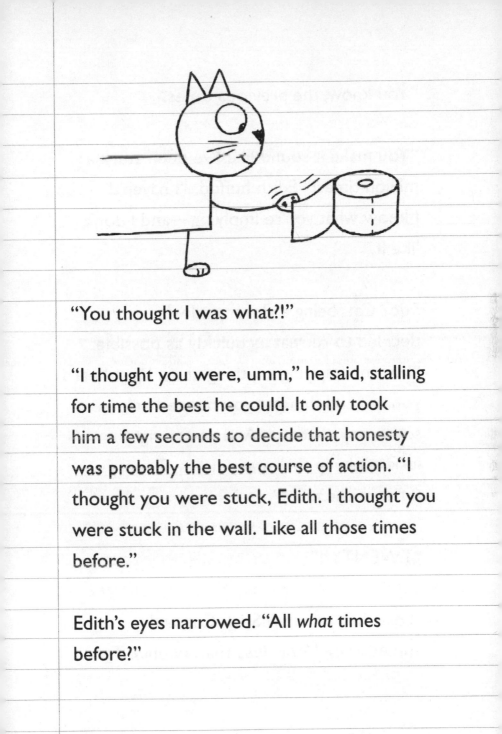

"You thought I was what?!"

"I thought you were, umm," he said, stalling for time the best he could. It only took him a few seconds to decide that honesty was probably the best course of action. "I thought you were stuck, Edith. I thought you were stuck in the wall. Like all those times before."

Edith's eyes narrowed. "All *what* times before?"

"You know, the previous times."

"You make it sound like I've been stuck a million times!" Edith huffed. "I haven't! I know what you're implying—and I don't like it."

Stick Cat, being a clever and wise cat, decided to retreat as quickly as possible. "I wasn't implying anything at all. I just heard you call and thought you needed help in some way, that's all. And you're right: it hasn't been that many times. Twenty times at the most."

"TWENTY?!"

"Less than twenty," Stick Cat said immediately. "Way less than twenty. Ten."

"TEN?!"

"Did I say ten?
I meant five.
No, three."

"Maybe three," Edith said, and un-squinted
her eyes.

"Probably even less than three."

"Probably," Edith said. She seemed satisfied
now.

One of the things that Stick Cat loved best
about Edith was how she could instantly do
something—whether it was fall asleep, get
over hurt feelings, or even jump from one
window ledge to another. And he was happy
that she suddenly seemed done with this

part of their conversation.

"Why were you calling me if you weren't—" he began, but then started again. "Why were you calling me?"

"Stick Cat, I was thinking about something this morning," Edith replied. "I was up on the kitchen counter after Tiffany left. She had a donut this morning. She left me some really tasty crumbs."

"That was nice of her," Stick Cat said.

"Tiffany always does nice things like that," Edith said. "Well, I was up on that counter after licking the plate. You know, just hanging around up there. And it reminded me of that time we were on Goose's counter after finding those blueberry muffin crumbs he left for us. Do you remember that?"

"I do," Stick Cat said. "Those were good."

"And I was thinking how nice it would have been to share those donut crumbs with you like you shared those blueberry muffin crumbs with me."

"Mm-hmm."

"I can't now, of course. Because I ate them all. You know how donut crumbs are. You can't eat just one. You have to keep going. There's absolutely no way to stop. So I'm not saying I actually *have* donut crumbs to share or anything."

"I understand."

"I just don't want you to think there are any donuts over here is all I'm saying. I'm simply saying I *thought* about sharing them. Not that I could. Because they're all gone. And not because I *chose* to eat them all. They're just donut crumbs and it's impossible *not* to eat them all once you've had a taste."

"I understand," Stick Cat said again.

Edith sat back on her hind legs and licked her front left paw as she continued to speak. She stopped to examine the placement of each strand of fur every now and then.

"So when I thought about sharing those crumbs with you—even though I can't—

something occurred to me," Edith said.

"What's that?"

"You've never been to my apartment, that's what!"

It was an intriguing thought to Stick Cat— for a couple of reasons. First, it had never occurred to him that he and Edith would spend the day at her apartment. It just seemed natural for *her* to come to *his* house. It was the way they had always done it. It was also intriguing to Stick Cat for another reason: Edith had thought of it and he hadn't.

"You know what?" he asked, and smiled. "You're right. I never have."

And with that Stick Cat began to climb into the bathroom cabinet. In just a few seconds he had climbed over the spare toilet paper rolls and begun to poke his head through the wall into Edith's apartment.

But he didn't make it any farther.

"Hey!" Edith shouted. "What are you doing?!"

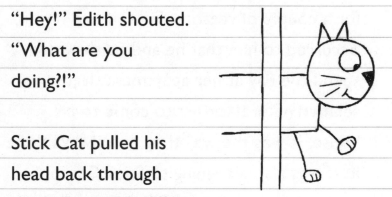

Stick Cat pulled his head back through the hole quickly. "I'm coming over."

"Humph!" Edith said, simultaneously closing her eyes and turning her head. "I don't think so, buster."

"Why not?"

"You weren't invited, that's
why not!"

"But I thought when you said—" Stick Cat
began and then stopped himself. He sat
down in the bathroom cabinet and looked
through the hole. He could see Edith sitting
there with her head still turned away from
him. Stick Cat figured the best thing he could
do was wait.

Finally, Edith spoke.

"Stick Cat?" she asked formally. Edith had
now turned to face him.

"Yes?"

"Would you like to come to my house today?"

An Invitation to StickCat from Edith

"I'd love to," he answered, and nodded. He came closer to the hole in the wall, but stopped one step short of it. "When would be a convenient time?"

"How sweet of you to ask," Edith answered. She seemed to appreciate this formal tone of voice from Stick Cat. "Right now would be fine."

"It would be an honor," Stick Cat said, and climbed through the hole, comfortable now that he would be welcomed completely.

Once he was in Edith's apartment, things became significantly more informal.

Edith led him out of the cabinet and into the bathroom, which looked exactly like Stick Cat's, except there was a green and yellow polka-dotted shower curtain instead of a plain blue one.

"Can I show you around?" Edith asked as they exited the bathroom.

"I'd like that."

Chapter 3

STEAK, SILK, AND CASHMERE

"Let's go to the kitchen first," Edith said, and padded off. Her head was held high and there was a certain, barely perceptible, strut in her gait. She was proud of the home that she let Tiffany share with her. Upon entering the kitchen, Edith continued, "Here it is. This is where Tiffany makes my breakfast."

Stick Cat looked around. Like the bathroom, this all seemed very familiar to him. There were only slight differences. The small table off to the side was circular instead of rectangular. The cabinets had different handles and the walls were painted light green instead of tan.

"It's very nice," commented Stick Cat. "When you say 'makes your breakfast,' what does that mean?"

"What do you mean, 'what does that mean?'"

"How does Tiffany 'make' your breakfast?" Stick Cat asked again. "Goose just tears open a pouch and pours my breakfast into my bowl. Isn't that what Tiffany does?"

STICK CAT
FOOD

For a single second, Edith looked at Stick Cat with shock. Quickly, however, she regained her composure even though it was clearly evident she found this whole idea quite primitive and unsavory.

She said, "Umm, Tiffany did that a few times for me when I was younger, but I made her stop."

"You made her stop?"

"That's right," Edith answered. Then she shook her head a bit and said, "I don't eat just any old thing that comes out of a plastic pouch. I have too sophisticated a palate for that."

"How did you make her stop?"

"I refused to eat it, that's how," Edith answered immediately. "And sometimes I would step on the edge of my bowl and tip it over. Then I'd walk out of the kitchen without eating a bite."

"Didn't you get hungry?"

"Of course I did. But it was a small price to pay," Edith answered. "Tiffany soon began serving me much better food."

"Like what?"

EDITH FOOD

"Oh, scrambled eggs. Bacon or sausage for breakfast usually," answered Edith. She sniffed the air in the kitchen now, attempting to pick up any lingering aromas to provide Stick Cat with a more comprehensive answer. "Then dinner is usually steak or salmon cut up into little pieces. I like rice with my dinner. I prefer basmati, but I'm not too picky. And there has to be a few drops of hot sauce on everything. I *LOVE* hot sauce. Especially on scrambled eggs."

"You do?"

"A lot!" Edith exclaimed. "I like things spicy. It matches my personality. I'm spicy, don't you think?"

Stick Cat smiled. "I do."

"Tiffany has a whole collection of different hot sauces just for me."

For some reason, he found it very unsurprising that Edith loved hot sauce.

"You should stop eating for Goose—that will change everything," Edith suggested. "You might even get some hot sauce!"

"I don't know," answered Stick Cat after a moment of consideration. This was all very, very strange to him. He had never been served anything besides pouch food. Goose was nice enough to change the flavors of his meals, but they always, always came from a pouch. For some reason, refusing to eat what was given to him just didn't seem like a very nice thing to do—even if it might lead to better food. "I don't mind the pouch food. Some of it's pretty tasty."

"Suit yourself," Edith said. "But you don't know what you're missing."

"Maybe you could save some of yours for me sometime?"

"I'd really like to, Stick Cat. I really would," Edith said, and sighed. "But here's the problem: Tiffany does this strange thing whenever she prepares my meals. It's always the perfect amount, the ideal portion. There's never one morsel left over."

"That's okay," Stick Cat said. He wanted to change the subject. "What else can you show me?"

"I can show you the bedroom," Edith said. She tilted her head toward the kitchen doorway. "Come on."

Stick Cat began to follow her. As he did, he glanced back toward Edith's food bowl. He noticed something he hadn't seen before.

"Why is there a pillow by your food bowl?"

"Oh, the tile floor gets so cold under my paws when I'm eating," Edith said without slowing down. "I made Tiffany get the pillow for me."

"How did you do that?"

"I stopped eating again," Edith said. "I get a lot of things that way. Eventually, Tiffany just keeps trying things to get me to eat again. She figured out the pillow thing in just a couple of days. She's fairly bright."

Stick Cat said nothing else as he followed Edith out of the kitchen, through the living room, and into the bedroom.

"Here's where I let Tiffany sleep with me," Edith said, and pointed up to a neatly made bed. There was a fluffy blanket decorated with yellow and white daisies folded halfway down the bed. On one side of the bed was a small table and lamp. On the other side, a rectangular pegboard was attached to the wall. It had Edith's bejeweled collars hanging on it. She had a different collar for each day of the week.

"It's very nice," Stick Cat said. Then, observing the pillows at the head of the bed, he commented, "Tiffany must use a lot of pillows. Goose only has two—and there are four here."

"No, no," Edith said. "She only uses one. The other three are mine."

Stick Cat tried not to act surprised. "You sleep with three pillows? And Tiffany sleeps with just one?"

"That's all she needs," Edith explained. While this didn't make much sense to Stick Cat, it all seemed perfectly logical to Edith. "And I like to move from one pillow to another before settling down to sleep. I never know which one is going to be just right on a particular night."

Stick Cat tilted his head to the right just a little and asked, "Aren't they all the same? They're all covered in that shiny pink material."

"That's silk. I only sleep with silk pillowcases. But they're not the same at all," Edith said, and then explained some more. "One pillow is a little softer. One is a little harder. And one is sort of medium. I never know which will be right until I try each one out a few times every night."

"Oh."

"Then, when I do figure out which one is best," Edith continued. She seemed to be taking enjoyment in describing her bedtime ritual. "That's when I let Tiffany tuck me in."

"Tuck you in?"

"That's right," Edith
answered. "She puts
that cashmere blanket
on me."

"She puts the blanket *over* you?"

"Of course," Edith answered. "Isn't that
what Goose does?"

"Umm, no."

"What do you do with *your* cashmere
blanket?"

"I lie on it, not under it," Stick Cat said.
This was all starting to make him feel funny
for some reason. He wasn't jealous of all

the luxuries Edith seemed to have. But he couldn't help wondering what steak and salmon tasted like—or what it felt like to have three silk-covered pillows and a cashmere blanket. "That's what most cats do, I think."

"Not this cat, mister," Edith said immediately. "I can't believe you sleep *on* your blanket instead of *under* it."

"Well, umm, it's not really a blanket anyway. Umm, yeah."

"What is it?"

"It's more like a towel."

"A bath towel?" Edith asked. She was just now realizing that maybe Stick Cat did not have a similar sleeping arrangement. "Well, that's okay, I guess. Those can be kind of soft and cushy sometimes. I'm sure it's quite comfortable."

"It's not a bath towel."

"It's not?"

"No."

"What kind of towel is it?"

"It's more like, umm, a dish towel."

"A dish towel?!"

"Mm-hmm."

"I see," Edith said.

Suddenly she seemed to be searching for words to use. "Well, those can be very nice. Especially if they're new."

"Mine's not new."

"It's not?"

"No. It's kind of old. It has some tears in the middle and it's kind of frayed on the ends," Stick Cat explained. He had always loved that towel. It was worn, yes, but it had always been his. It was familiar and cozy. "Goose was going to throw it away, but then he decided to put it in my box."

"Your BOX?!"

Stick Cat nodded.

"You sleep in a *BOX*?!"

"Yes. Sometimes, I'll jump up into bed with Goose in the morning, but I prefer the box. It's right by the side of Goose's bed. I'm sure you've seen it."

"I guess I've never noticed."

"It's not my favorite place to sleep," added Stick Cat. "It's just where I sleep most often."

"Where's your favorite place?"

"Goose's lap, of course," Stick Cat said. "Isn't your favorite place to sleep Tiffany's lap?"

"No way. Too hot!" Edith exclaimed. "She's always trying to get me onto her lap. But I prefer my three pillows, silk pillowcases, and cashmere blanket by far."

"Have you always had all those things?" Stick Cat asked.

Edith shook her head. "No, not always."

"How did you get them?"

"I stopped sleeping," Edith explained as they walked out of the bedroom. "I would just get up in the middle of the night and move around. Eventually, it drove Tiffany crazy. And that's when she started trying out new things to help me sleep. It's just another one of the ways I've trained her. She's a pretty fast learner."

Stick Cat was growing tired of Edith's explanations. He couldn't imagine acting that way with Goose. Edith's way of doing things made him feel uncomfortable.

He scanned Edith's living room as they entered it. He saw the morning sunshine streaming through the glass. And he saw a very inviting windowsill.

Chapter 4

A WHOLE NEW VIEW

Stick Cat did not
hesitate in hopping
up to the sill to gaze
out the window.

"Umm, excuse me,"
Edith huffed.

"Yes?" Stick Cat answered. He peered out
the window at the building across the alley.
It had never even occurred to Stick Cat that
Edith's apartment would have a completely
different view. It was instantly fascinating to
him.

"What are you doing?"

Stick Cat continued to stare. "I'm looking out the window. That brick building across the alley is so neat. You can see the roof and everything!"

"That's not what I mean," Edith said, and came two steps closer.

Stick Cat knew this tone of voice. He asked, "What is it? Is something the matter?"

Edith said nothing until she crossed the living room completely and stood right next to the windowsill.

"You didn't *ask* if you could sit up there," Edith said. She didn't sound rude or mean. It sounded more like she was reminding Stick

Cat of something. "It is my windowsill after all."

Now, Stick Cat might have reminded Edith of something himself. He might have reminded her that she had hopped up onto *his* windowsill in *his* apartment dozens—no, hundreds—of times. And she had never asked before.

But he didn't.

Stick Cat knew how to handle this with Edith. He had experience.

Stick Cat jumped down.

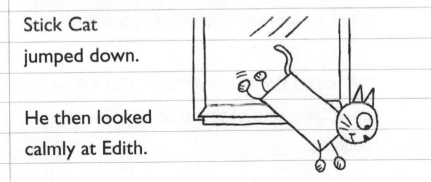

He then looked calmly at Edith.

In a completely normal voice, he asked, "May I hop up on your windowsill and look outside?"

Edith smiled. "Oh, Stick Cat," she said. "You didn't even have to ask. You're always welcome."

Stick Cat jumped back up and gazed again at all the new things out the window. The first thing he saw was very close to the window—right outside it actually.

"Why are there stairs outside your window?" he asked.

Edith answered, "That's a fire escape."

"What's a fire escape?" Stick Cat asked. "I don't have one of those on my side of the building."

"If there's a fire in the middle of the night, I can wake up, open the window, and walk down the steps to safety," explained Edith.

"You and Tiffany, you mean."

"Me and Tiffany?" asked Edith. She seemed puzzled.

"Yes. If you were sleeping and there was a fire, you *and* Tiffany would climb down to safety, right?"

"Well, I suppose if she woke up too."

"But wouldn't you wake her up?"

"In the middle of a fire?! Are you kidding?" Edith was truly flabbergasted. She hopped up to the sill to join Stick Cat. "Hey, in this apartment it's every woman for herself."

Stick Cat waited a long moment. He was ready to change the subject again. "It's so neat to see the roof of that building. And there's a little garden!"

"Hmm," Edith said. She was completely disinterested. To Stick Cat it was all new, fascinating, and spectacular. To Edith, not so much.

Stick Cat continued to stare in absolute wonder. He had never seen the top of a building so close before. He and Edith lived on the twenty-third floor. But on Stick Cat's side, the building across the alley was much taller. On Edith's side, however, the building next door was one floor shorter than their level—twenty-two floors high.

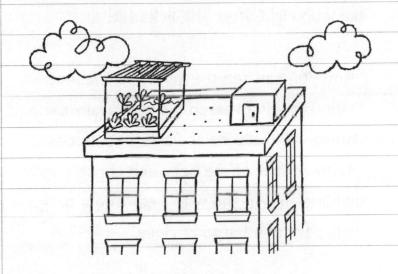

So, to see a roof like this—and so close— was incredibly interesting.

"Look at those flowers in the garden," Stick Cat said. "I can see daisies and black-eyed Susans. So pretty."

"Yeah, I guess," Edith commented without looking up. She licked her front left paw. There was  a single stubborn strand of fur that popped back up right after she licked it.

"And you can see the river!" exclaimed Stick Cat. He pressed his face against the window and stared as far left as he could. "Through the space between those two buildings down the way. I can see a barge— well, part of a barge anyway."

"Hmm," Edith said with complete disinterest. The 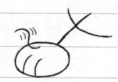 strand of fur popped up again. She licked it once more. "Never noticed."

"And the sky! You can see a huge patch

of sky!" Stick Cat nearly yelled. His eyes stretched wide open. "I was so busy looking at the roof and the garden that I didn't even notice. Because the building across the alley is shorter, you can see so much more sky! It's just beautiful today."

Edith did not look up. That fur strand had popped up again. She used her front right paw to pat it down.

Stick Cat said, "I had no idea you have such an incredible view of the sky."

Edith placed her right paw over her left paw—and over that annoying strand of fur. It seemed as if she decided to just cover it up. That way, she wouldn't have to look at it.

She finally lifted her head and asked, "What are you going on and on about, Stick Cat?"

"The sky," he answered. "It's beautiful."

"The sky? Seriously?"

Stick Cat just nodded, never turning his head away from the window.

"It's just the sky, Stick Cat," Edith said. "I mean, it's there almost every day."

"*Almost* every day?"

"Yes, that's what I said. Almost every day."

"Not every day?"

"Some days I don't look out the window," Edith said in an attempt to explain things better.

"But that doesn't mean the sky's not there."

"It's not there for me, mister."

Stick Cat pondered Edith's words for a few minutes. Sometimes, he decided, it was better to not say anything at all. He turned toward Edith after that decision and asked, "What's the deal with that woman on the top floor?"

"That's Hazel," Edith answered without

looking at Stick Cat. Instead, she lowered her chin down to the sill and stared at her front paws. She slowly lifted her right paw off her left one and peeked underneath. She tried to see if that fur strand would pop up again.

To Edith's great relief it did not pop up. She gave a great exhale of air.

"Who is Hazel?" asked Stick Cat.

"She makes the bagels."

"What bagels?"

"There's a shop down on the street called Hazel's Bagels," Edith explained. "My roommate, Tiffany, gets them for us on Saturday mornings. Hazel cooks them up on that top floor and then takes them down to the shop."

"You eat bagels?"

"On Saturdays, yes," Edith said nonchalantly. She seemed to think everyone in the city ate bagels on Saturday mornings.

"I've never tried a bagel before," Stick Cat said. He didn't sound disappointed. He was simply stating a fact.

"They're okay," Edith commented. "But it's really what comes with them that I like."

"What comes with them?"

"Lox and cream cheese," Edith answered. She had become instantly excited. "I *LOVE* lox!"

"What are lox?"

"I don't know," Edith answered honestly. "It's pink and it tastes like fish, but it's not. It's soft and mushy and salty."

"Sounds good," Stick Cat said.

Stick Cat watched Hazel move around

inside the brick building across the alley. He asked, "What's she doing?"

"She's just doing what she does every morning. I've watched her a million times."

Edith took a long, deep inhale of air. She double-checked to ensure that stubborn fur strand had not sprung back up. Then she, like Stick Cat, cast her gaze across the alley at Hazel.

Hazel herself was an older woman with gray, curly hair. She was skinny and a little frail-looking. She had a smile on her face—as if she was content to be at a job she liked. She appeared happy to be making bagels this morning.

"The first thing she does is drink some

coffee and open the window," began Edith. She wriggled herself into a comfortable position next to Stick Cat. "You can't make bagels without drinking coffee and opening the window. I've learned that."

You could tell this observation struck Stick Cat as a little strange, but he didn't comment about it. He asked, "What's next?"

"Then she dumps the cloud bags into the giant bucket."

Stick Cat could see the huge bucket that Edith referred to. It looked more like a huge cooking pot to him. It was the same shape as the big pot Goose used every few months to make a batch of chili or soup or stew. Hazel's pot was about one hundred times the size. It was much taller than Hazel herself.

A stepladder stood next to the pot. Stick Cat rightly assumed that Hazel climbed the ladder to pour the ingredients into the pot.

"What are cloud bags?"

"Those huge bags on the shelf over there," Edith said, and pointed. "She opens about ten of them and pours the cloud powder into the giant bucket. Whenever she does, it always creates this big powdery cloud. It's my favorite part of the process."

"Why?"

"You'll see."

"What's she doing now?" Stick Cat asked.

Hazel had set her coffee cup down on a rung of the ladder. She walked toward a sink on the far wall, turned the faucet on, and dragged a hose from the sink to the pot.

"She has to fill the giant bucket with water first," Edith said. "She fills it about halfway. Then it's cloud powder time. Then stirring. After that, she scoops this thick stuff out of the bucket and starts shaping the bagels on that silver table. She makes thousands of them at that table with the bagel sign hanging over it."

They watched in silence as Hazel stood on the ladder and sprayed water into the pot. Every now and then Hazel put her hand in the running water to test the temperature. She bent down

occasionally to grab her coffee cup and take a sip before placing it back on the ladder.

"So she starts stirring the water and cloud powder together next?" asked Stick Cat.

Edith didn't answer.

There was a good reason for that.

She was asleep.

Stick Cat smiled at her. He took real pleasure in knowing that he would sit there on the windowsill and see a whole new view of the big city. New buildings. New windows. A new patch of sky. Different streets twenty-three stories below.

He stretched a little, careful not to nudge Edith and wake her. He rested his head on his paws and set about taking in this whole new, exciting view.

But it only lasted seven minutes.

In seven minutes, everything about Stick Cat's peaceful day would change.

Chapter 5

THE DISAPPEARANCE

Edith snored.

Stick Cat watched.

And Hazel continued to make the bagels.
The pot now had enough water and she
had returned the hose to the sink. The next
step in the bagel-making process fascinated
Stick Cat.

He understood now what Edith meant by
"cloud powder." Each time Hazel dumped
one of the large, heavy bags into the pot, a
cloud of fine white powder erupted. Even

though she was near the
top of the stepladder
next to the pot, a white
cloud would billow up and
cover Hazel each time she
emptied a bag.

While Hazel continued to
dump the bags, Stick Cat
relaxed and took in the view. He stretched
to look left down to the river again. The
barge was now gone, but a steel-blue
tugboat chugged slowly
through the water. A flash
of red caught Stick Cat's
eye and he snapped his head
toward the garden on the
roof of the building across
the alley.

A cardinal was perched on a vine-covered trellis along the side of the garden. Stick Cat had never seen a cardinal before. He had only seen pigeons and, sometimes, seagulls from his window. This bright red cardinal fascinated him. It was smaller than any bird he had ever seen—and far more colorful. It swooped down to the garden, pecked about on the soil for several seconds, and then flew back up to its trellis perch. It did this several times before flying halfway to Stick Cat and landing on the thick black cable that hung between the two buildings.

CABLE TELEVISION - NO ELECTRICITY

The cable wiggled and twitched when the cardinal landed on it, catching Stick Cat's attention. The cable connected to the wall above Edith's window and ran across the alley to Hazel's building, where it attached above her open window. On its rubber casing the words "Cable Television—No Electricity" were printed.

The cable twitched again when the cardinal spread its wings, dropped from its perch, and flew out of sight. Stick Cat hoped he would see it again.

As Edith slept, Stick Cat watched Hazel progress through her bagel-making steps. She had already dumped seven bags of cloud powder into the huge pot filled with water. He watched as she dumped four more and then rested. The bags looked so heavy. Stick

Cat was not surprised she needed to rest.

Hazel sat on the top step of the ladder
breathing heavily. Stick Cat glanced at Edith
next to him—she breathed heavily too. Her
eyes were closed and there was a hint of a
grin on her face.

Hazel took two big sips of coffee as she sat
there for a moment to regain her strength.

It didn't take long.
In just a couple of
minutes she set her
cup down. Some
coffee sloshed and
spilled, but Hazel didn't seem to notice. She
climbed down three steps to reach a long
wooden paddle that leaned against the pot.
It looked like a canoe paddle.

Hazel climbed back up, stuck the paddle's bigger side into the pot, and began to stir. Stick Cat noticed that it was an effortless motion for the first minute or so. As Hazel continued to stir, however, it seemed to get harder and harder. It was as if the substance in the pot—the combination of cloud powder and water—became thicker and thicker.

As the pot ingredients thickened, Hazel moved up one step so she could reach farther into the pot. In just a few minutes she was on the third highest step. She bent over the pot, reaching farther and farther into it.

It looked like she was close to done. There was a little smile on her face. She brushed some moist gray hair from her forehead. Stick Cat looked forward to watching the next part of Hazel's routine—shaping the bagels into circles.

There was something special about Hazel that Stick Cat liked. She seemed so determined—and content—in her work. She liked making bagels. Stick Cat thought there was probably genuine satisfaction in making something that people loved to eat. Maybe there were customers who made special trips across the big city just to get one of Hazel's bagels. He thought she must take tremendous pride in serving those customers down at the street-level store.

The bagel batter was now thicker than ever,

Stick Cat could tell. It seemed to grow more dense as every minute passed. Now Hazel's arms were tense. He could see her thin muscles flex as she pulled the paddle through the thick batter.

Hazel moved one step higher—the second highest rung on the ladder. She pushed the paddle into the furthest reaches of the pot. She leaned forward. Hazel plunged the paddle deeper and then pulled it toward her.

Then the entire motion turned backward.

Hazel was no longer pulling the paddle toward herself.

It was as if the paddle—mired and stuck and stubborn in that thick bagel batter—now pulled Hazel toward it.

And then Hazel disappeared.

Chapter 6

BEACH BALLS AND FLIPPERS

It took Stick Cat only a few seconds to realize what had happened. Hazel had slipped in the spilled coffee and fallen into the pot.

Stick Cat could feel his heart speed up and thump hard inside his chest. He stood up on the windowsill and pressed against the glass, waiting for Hazel to climb out of the pot.

She didn't come out.

Stick Cat waited.

She didn't come out.

Stick Cat couldn't wait any longer.

"Edith!" Stick Cat yelled urgently. "Edith, wake up! There's an emergency!"

Only Edith's eyelids moved. The rest of her body remained perfectly still and calm. It was as if only her eyes had awoken while the rest of her body stayed in a perfect state of slumber. She didn't speak, but answered simply by shifting her eyes to look at Stick Cat.

"It's Hazel!" Stick Cat yelled. "She fell into the bagel pot!"

Edith closed her eyes.

"Edith!"

This time her mouth was the only body part that moved. Her eyes stayed closed. She calmly asked, "What is it, Stick Cat?"

"Hazel! Trouble! She fell in!"

"Fell into what?" Edith sighed.

"The bagel pot!" Stick Cat yelled. "She fell
off the ladder! She hasn't come out!"

"Maybe she's going for a swim," Edith
suggested, maintaining her complete sense of
calm and absolute lack of motion.

"A swim?!"

"Sure," Edith said. "Humans like to swim. I
don't get it, to be honest. It just messes up
their hair. It's like taking a shower or a bath.
Why would anyone want to mess up their
hair? People are crazy."

Stick Cat tried to calm his racing heart. He

took three deep breaths and exhaled the air as slowly as he could.

"Edith," he said. "I need you to wake up! Hazel's in big trouble. I think the stuff in the pot—the cloud powder and the water mixture—is so thick that she can't pull herself out."

At this, Edith finally opened her eyes and turned toward Stick Cat.

"Did I miss the cloud powder part?"

Stick Cat nodded.

"I love it when she gets covered in cloud powder!" Edith said, and giggled. "Doesn't she look totally ridiculous? It's so funny!"

"Umm, yeah. I guess," Stick Cat said.

Edith giggled some more as she remembered past times when Hazel had been covered by white powder. "It's like the cloud just explodes on her!" Edith exclaimed, and laughed even harder. "She instantly looks like a ghost or something."

"Edith," Stick Cat said. "I don't think you understand the gravity of the situation. It's serious! Hazel's in danger!"

"I told you, she probably just went for a swim."

"In a big pot of that stuff?!"

"Sure, why not?" Edith answered. "Let me ask you this, Stick Cat: Was Hazel wearing a bikini when she dove in?"

Stick Cat stared at Edith for a few seconds. "No. She wasn't wearing a bikini. And she didn't 'dive' in. She fell in."

"Did she have a beach ball?"

"A beach ball?"

"Yes, a beach ball," Edith answered. "People always take beach balls when they go swimming."

"Umm, no. She didn't have a beach ball."

Edith stood up on the windowsill and stretched her back into an arch. She glanced out the window at the sky.

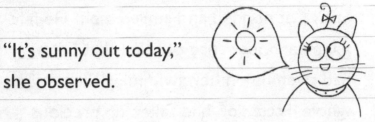

"It's sunny out today," she observed.

"Umm," Stick Cat said. "It is, yes."

"People always go swimming when it's sunny."

This had become too much—even for Stick Cat. He tried to compose himself. He took three deep breaths again. He rotated his shoulders a bit in an attempt to release the tension he felt there. As calmly as he could, Stick Cat said, "She's not swimming, Edith."

After a moment, Edith conceded.

"Okay, okay," she said. "Maybe she isn't swimming after all."

Stick Cat nodded and smiled a bit. He felt a tremendous sense of relief that Edith had given up on her swimming theory. The whole discussion had taken up precious time.

"Okay," he began to declare. "Now we need to—"

But he was interrupted by Edith.

"Maybe she's scuba diving."

Stick Cat lowered his head and studied the wood grain of the windowsill.

He silently counted
to five in his mind.

Edith asked, "Was
she wearing any oxygen tanks on her back?"

Stick Cat didn't answer. He counted to five
again.

"Or flippers?"

He counted to five again.

"Or a snorkel?"

He counted to five.

"Stick Cat?" Edith asked. "Is something
wrong?"

Stick Cat finally—and slowly—raised his head. "I'm fine," he answered. "And I just want you to know how much I appreciate your thoughts and ideas about what happened to Hazel. I truly believe you're the only one in the whole world who could come up with such ideas."

"Well, thank you, Stick Cat," Edith said. She looked away and smiled to herself. You could tell she took Stick Cat's words as quite a compliment indeed.

"Great ideas, for sure," Stick Cat reiterated. Then the spark of an idea came into his mind. He asked, "But since there was no bikini, beach ball, oxygen tanks, flippers, or snorkel, what do you think she could be doing in there?"

"You know what?" Edith said. It was as if an idea had suddenly occurred to her. Her eyes flashed open wider. She leaned closer toward the window and peered across the alley. "Maybe she fell in."

Stick Cat snapped his head toward Edith. His mouth was agape. "I think you might be right."

Edith nodded knowingly. She licked the back of her left front paw and rubbed it across her left eyebrow. *"Might* be right?"

Stick Cat immediately said, "You *are* right, Edith. I'm sure of it."

By this time, something had happened across the alley that neither Stick Cat nor Edith had noticed.

Two frail, pale, batter-covered hands had reached out from inside the big pot and gripped the rim.

Hazel was trying to get out.

But she didn't stand a chance.

Not by herself.

Chapter 7

FOR THE LOVE OF LOX

"We have to get over there!" Stick Cat exclaimed.

"Over where?" Edith said, and flopped back down on the windowsill. She wriggled a bit to get into a comfortable resting position.

"Across the alley to save Hazel!"

 "Oh, Stick Cat, Stick Cat," Edith said, and closed her eyes. "We've already rescued one person. Don't you remember? What was

his name? Mr. Tambourine Man or something?"

"Mr. Music."

"Right, right. Mr. Music," Edith said, and nodded her head as much as she could, considering her chin rested comfortably on the windowsill. "We've already rescued *him*. We can't go rescuing someone *else*."

"Why not?" Stick Cat asked. He snapped his head back and forth between Edith and the window.

"Well, it would just be so selfish, that's why," Edith said, and yawned. She appeared to be seriously considering a second nap. "We should let a couple of other cats have a turn."

Stick Cat knew he couldn't do this alone. The truth was, he didn't even think he could do it with Edith. But together, he figured they might have a chance.

A tiny chance.

They had to get across the alley to the other building. And this time there was nothing as convenient as an apron and a clothesline like when they rescued Mr. Music. As scary as that had been, at least Stick Cat could reel the line and move them across and back. There was nothing like that here.

A single black cable stretched between the two buildings.

That was it.

There was nothing else.

He had to think of something—and fast.
But first he had to contend with Edith. How
could he convince her to help rescue Hazel?

How?

And then Stick Cat squinted one eye for a
fraction of a second. He turned to Edith.
Her eyes were closed, but she wasn't
snoring yet.

"Hey, Edith," he said.

"Mm-hmm?"

"What are those pink things that come with bagels?"

"Lox."

"Oh, right. Lox," Stick Cat said. He had now noticed Hazel's hands—only her hands—on the rim of the humongous pot. Every minute or two she would reposition them. She was hanging on—not climbing out—of the pot. Stick Cat *had* to get over there. "And what do those lox taste like?"

Edith smiled a bit before answering. She licked her lips. "Like fish. Soft and chewy.

Sort of smoky. A little bit salty. And that flavor—that smoky, salty, fishy flavor—lingers in your mouth for a little while."

"They sound delicious," Stick Cat said.

"Oh, they're scrumptious," Edith sighed. "Just scrumptious."

Stick Cat waited. He watched Hazel's hands. She seemed to be holding on for the time being.

"Scrumptious," Edith repeated, and sighed again.

Stick Cat held still.

And then Edith made the sound that Stick Cat had been waiting for.

It wasn't snoring.

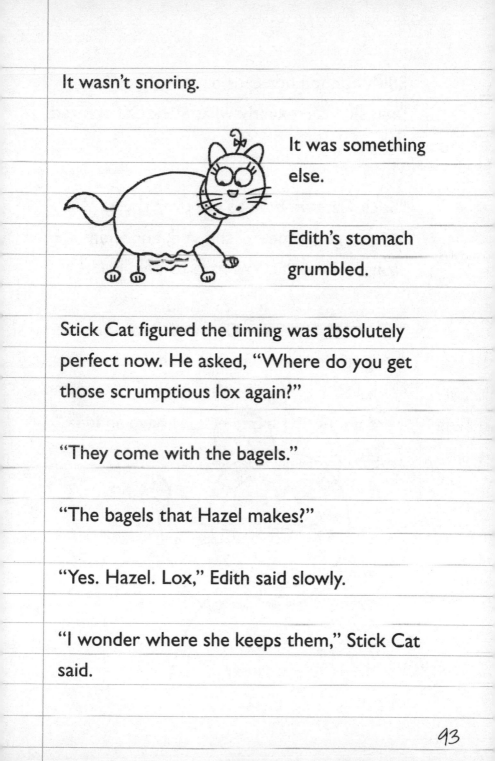

It was something else.

Edith's stomach grumbled.

Stick Cat figured the timing was absolutely perfect now. He asked, "Where do you get those scrumptious lox again?"

"They come with the bagels."

"The bagels that Hazel makes?"

"Yes. Hazel. Lox," Edith said slowly.

"I wonder where she keeps them," Stick Cat said.

Edith opened her eyes quickly then. And then she said exactly what Stick Cat wanted to hear.

"Stick Cat, we *have* to get over there. We have to get some—" she said, and then stopped herself. "We have to help Hazel."

"You're right," Stick Cat said. "How are we going to do that?"

"I have an idea."

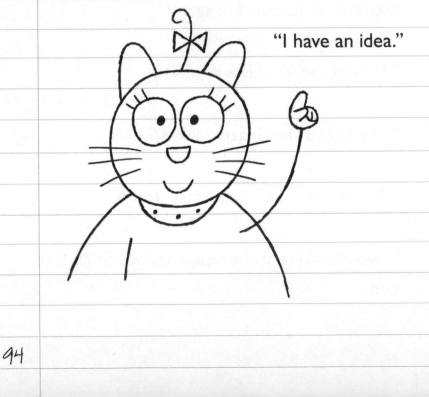

Chapter 8

CRUMBS AND PARACHUTES

"You have an idea to help Hazel?!" Stick Cat asked. He was obviously surprised that Edith had already come up with an alley-crossing rescue plan.

"You betcha," Edith said.

"Okay, then," Stick Cat said. "What do we do?"

"We use parachutes."

"Parachutes?"

"Parachutes."

Now, Stick Cat didn't know quite how to address this idea. He knew what parachutes were—big pieces of material that caught air beneath them and allowed the user to float down to the ground with a soft landing.

But Stick Cat also knew a couple of other things about parachutes. First, they tended to float *down*, not *across*. If he and Edith used parachutes they would likely drift down to the alley—or, even worse, down and out a bit into the city traffic.

Even more important, Stick Cat knew one vital fact.

Do you know what it was?

I'll tell you.

Stick Cat knew they didn't have any parachutes.

"Great idea, Edith," Stick Cat said after thinking about his response for a moment. "Unfortunately, we don't have any parachutes."

"Oh, Stick Cat," Edith said, and sighed. "Do I have to do everything? Do I have to come up with the excellent idea to get across the alley and get some lox—I mean, umm, try to help Hazel? And do I *also* have to come up with the supplies to execute my excellent plan? Can't you do that part at least?"

"I'm sorry, Edith," Stick Cat answered. "I forgot to bring parachutes with me today."

Edith said nothing as she stared down at the windowsill. "It's okay, Stick Cat," Edith said. "I'll take care of it."

And with that, Edith hopped down from the sill and began padding her way across the living room to the kitchen.

"Where are you going?"

Edith didn't even look back when she answered, "To get some parachutes."

Stick Cat was dumbfounded as he watched Edith disappear into the kitchen.

Could Edith actually have parachutes in the kitchen? It seemed impossible. But she had answered with such complete confidence. He almost believed she would emerge from the kitchen doorway with two parachutes in tow.

He waited.

And waited.

"Edith?" he called.

No answer.

He called louder. "Edith!"

"Yes?" she called back. Her voice sounded kind of mumbly or something.

"Are you coming back?"

"In a minute."

"With parachutes?"

"In a minute."

Stick Cat decided to investigate. He hopped quietly down to the carpet and moved across the living room. When he got to the kitchen doorway, Stick Cat stopped and peeked around its edge.

He could see Edith.

Well, he could see most of Edith.

Her four legs straddled the kitchen sink. Her head was out of sight— bent low into the sink. Stick Cat cocked his head a bit to listen. He could hear the distinct sound of a feline's rough-textured tongue lapping against a dish in the sink.

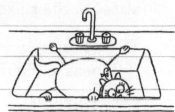

"Edith?"

She snapped her head up and out of the sink. Stick Cat could see donut crumbs on her lips and scattered about in her whiskers. She must have found some more on the plates in the sink.

"Hi," was all Edith said when she saw Stick Cat.

Stick Cat tried hard not to smile. Edith looked so guilty. He knew he had to hurry her out of the kitchen and find some way—any way—across the alley to help Hazel.

But this thing with Edith at the sink, he just *had* to inquire about it for a few seconds.

He asked, "What are you doing in the sink?"

"Umm," Edith said, and paused. She looked down into the sink. She discreetly licked a crumb from her whiskers—flicking her tongue in and out of her mouth quickly.

"What?"

"The sink," Stick Cat said, and stepped into the kitchen. "What are you doing in there?"

He could tell Edith was having trouble coming up with an answer—or an answer she wanted to share with Stick Cat anyway.

"Speak up, Stick Cat," she said. She seemed to be stalling for time. "I can't hear you."

Stick Cat knew what Edith was up to. He didn't care. He actually found it amusing. He stepped even closer—and spoke even louder. "What are you doing in the sink?"

Edith looked away. She held perfectly still for three seconds and then her shoulders twitched. Stick Cat could tell that she suddenly had an answer for him.

"I was looking for donut crumbs to give you, Stick Cat," she said. Edith grinned and licked her lips. "But there weren't any in here."

"None?"

"None."

"Zero?"

"Zero."

Stick Cat smiled. It would have been fun, he knew, to continue the conversation.

He wasn't even hungry and he didn't mind at all that Edith had not shared her crumbs with him. But the vision of Hazel's pale, frail hands gripping the rim of that bagel-batter pot kept dancing in his mind. He had to get over there. He had to help.

"Well, thanks for checking for donut crumbs for me, Edith," he said. "That was very kind of you."

Edith exhaled. She was visibly relieved. Without even noticing she did it, Edith licked the final crumb from her whiskers and said, "Well, I'm all about kindness, Stick Cat."

"Yes, I know," he said, and walked closer. "Didn't you come in here to get a couple of parachutes?"

"Yes," Edith answered. She pulled herself slowly and delicately from the sink. She might have thought if she went slowly Stick Cat would forget she was in the sink in the first place.

"Where are they?"

"Where are what?"

"The parachutes."

Edith continued to move in that slow, purposeful way. She took three steps away from the sink, reached below the counter, and pulled a small drawer open. "They're right here," she said. "That's the reason—the only reason—I came up on the counter."

Stick Cat needed to keep things moving. He said, "Great! Let's see them."

And with that Edith reached into that small drawer and pulled out two square pieces of cloth. She dropped them down to the kitchen floor.

"Those are, umm, napkins," Stick Cat said.

"They are napkins if you wipe your face with them," Edith said. She hopped down from the counter. "They're parachutes if you hold them above your head and jump out the window."

Stick Cat tilted his head just a bit. He stared at Edith. She sensed his confusion and tried to explain things more clearly to him.

"I think the trick," Edith said, "is to catch some air beneath the parachute before you jump."

"How do you do that?" Stick Cat asked. He didn't think the napkin would work as a parachute. In fact, he was absolutely positive about it. But he thought it would be polite to listen.

 "It's simple, really," answered Edith. She sounded completely sure of herself. "You hold a corner in one paw and then sort of toss it

gently over to the other paw."

She demonstrated this technique a few times. The napkin did actually catch a little air beneath it.

"As soon as you catch that other end," Edith went on, "you jump. As you fall, even more air gets trapped and you settle—ever so gently—to the ground."

"Umm," Stick Cat said. He could truly think of nothing else to say.

"Here, let's test it," Edith said with casual confidence. There was no doubt in her mind whatsoever. She picked up one of the napkins with her mouth and padded briskly to the living room.

Stick Cat held his position there in the kitchen for several seconds. He looked down at the remaining napkin on the floor. Did Edith really think these flimsy squares of material could somehow suspend them in the air as they floated across the alley to help Hazel? The whole notion—the whole idea—was preposterous. He knew that they were way too heavy. He knew they would instantly plummet to the alley twenty-three floors below.

Stick Cat reached down and picked up the napkin. He hustled out to the living room to catch up to Edith. He figured she was up on the couch preparing to test her parachute theory.

When he exited the kitchen and entered

the living room, he could see Edith clearly.

She wasn't on the couch.

The window was wide open. She was outside on the fire escape railing. She balanced there on her hind legs.

She bent her rear legs a bit and looked back over her shoulder at Stick Cat. She held a corner of the napkin in one paw and flicked it up into the air. She called just one thing to him.

"Watch this!"

And then Edith jumped.

Chapter 9

ZIPPING

You would think that Stick Cat would rush to the window, right?

He didn't.

He knew Edith was gone.

A flood of sadness washed over him. He remembered the first day they met— the exact moment their scratching had finally made a hole in the wall. He could see Edith's face through that hole—the fluffiness of her, the bow in her fur. He knew at that first moment they would become true friends. He wouldn't be alone all day when Goose went to work. He'd share each of those days with Edith.

But not anymore.

He hung his head.

For six seconds.

That's when Edith's voice came pouring through the open window.

"I told you it would work, Stick Cat!"

Stick Cat jerked his head up and sprang across the living room in two great, joyous bounds. He jumped to the windowsill.

Edith was halfway across the alley. The napkin-parachute was working.

Sort of.

Edith turned her head over her shoulder, saw Stick Cat on the windowsill of her apartment, and yelled again, "I told you!"

Do you know what zip lines are? They are these cool things that hold you suspended in the air while you zoom across a line from a higher elevation to a lower one. Stick Cat had never heard of zip lines, but he could certainly see how one worked. He watched Edith slide along the thick black cable across the alley to Hazel's window ledge.

It took Stick Cat just a few seconds to figure out what had happened.

As she had prepared to jump from the fire escape railing, Edith had held on to one corner of the napkin and flicked it to her other paw to get some air under it—just like she had demonstrated in the kitchen.

When she did, the napkin looped over the single black cable that ran across the alley. She jumped and glided down the cable—like on a zip line.

Stick Cat stared at
her in amazement.

Edith swung her paws from
side to side, reveling in the thrill
of the experience.

Stick Cat watched as she landed on the
windowsill across the alley—one floor
below where he stood. When she got
there, she released the napkin, stretched
her arms a bit, and turned to stare at him.

"Come on!" she called, and waved. "It's a
blast!"

Stick Cat looked down.

Twenty-three floors down.

"What are you waiting for?!" Edith called.

He hopped off the windowsill, retrieved his own napkin, and came back.

Edith saw him return and yelled across again. "You're going to love it! It's absolutely to die for!"

"That's what I'm afraid of," whispered Stick Cat.

"What?" called Edith across the alley. "Did you say something?"

"No. Nothing," Stick Cat answered.

Sorry. Need to pause here. I know it's a suspenseful part of the story and everything. I want to see if Stick Cat makes it across too. But we need to talk about this for a minute.

You know not to try your own homemade zip-line experiment, right? I mean, don't tie something to your bedpost on the second floor of your house and then tie the other end to your mailbox. Don't try to slide from your window down to the ground.

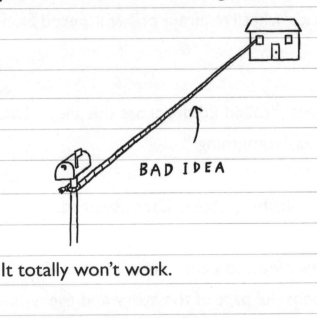

BAD IDEA

It totally won't work.

You're too heavy. You'd crash.

So no do-it-yourself zip-lining, okay?

Cool. Thanks.

Now let's see if Stick Cat gets across the alley.

He took his napkin and tossed one end up and over the thick black cable. Stick Cat clenched both ends, sticking his claws into the material. He thought if the napkin was strong enough to hold Edith, then it would be strong enough to hold him. He, of course, didn't mention this thought to Edith.

"Let's go already!" called Edith.

Stick Cat double-checked his grip on the napkin, looked across the alley—and pushed off the window ledge with all the strength he had in his back legs. He kept his eyes fixed on Edith, refusing to glance down.

"Look down!" called Edith. "It's totally awesome!"

Stick Cat stared at Edith.

"Not at me! Down!"

He was not going to look down.

"Down!"

Stick Cat got closer. He was more than
halfway across now. The wind rushed
past his face. His claws were firmly set.
The material didn't rip at all. He began
to feel confident—not comfortable, but
confident—that he would make it. He and
Edith could try to help Hazel. His confidence
grew as each second passed and his
remaining journey got shorter and shorter.

Until he stopped.

He was still at least thirty
feet from Edith. He swayed
a little but didn't move
forward at all.

"Stick Cat?" Edith asked.
She didn't need to speak as
loudly now.

"Y-yes?" There was a slight quiver in his voice.

"Why'd you stop?"

"I didn't s-stop on purpose."

"I wish I could have stopped," Edith said. There was genuine regret in her voice. "It's so fun out there, isn't it?"

"F-fun isn't quite the w-word I would use."

"You're talking funny," Edith said. "You sound all shaky or something. Are you cold?"

"Umm, n-no."

Stick Cat shifted his weight a little left and

right in an attempt to get moving again.

It didn't work.

Edith lay down on the window ledge.
You could tell she thought this might be a
while. Her tail and
one leg drooped
over the side and
dangled in the air.
She didn't seem to
notice at all.

"How long are you going to be, Stick Cat?"

He swayed a little harder but moved
forward only an inch or two. "Hopefully,
n-not too l-long," he answered.

"Why are you shifting around like that?"

"I'm trying t-to get m-moving again," he said. His arms and shoulders were growing sore and tired. He didn't know how much longer he could hold on.

"Oh."

Stick Cat closed his eyes, trying to gather his energy and strengthen his stamina. He took a deep breath and opened his eyes, ready to start scooching forward a few inches at a time again.

But when he opened his eyes, Stick Cat saw something he didn't want to see at all. Edith was up now and reaching toward the cable.

"What are you doing?!" he asked quickly.

"Just going to help,"
Edith said casually,
and grasped the black
cable in her front paws.
"Speed this along a bit."

Before Stick Cat could
shout "No!" Edith began to shake the cable
with all her might, yanking and jerking it in
every direction she could.

Instantly, Stick Cat began to swish and swing
about. His back legs and feet shot out wildly
in every direction. His torso whipped one
way while his hips thrashed another way. He
twisted and turned. He shook and shimmied.

But two very important things didn't change
position at all.

His front paws.

His claws dug into that material. His grip
never loosened.

And he started to move.

He began to slide toward Edith again. She
saw this movement, ceased yanking on
the cable, and nodded her head—more to
herself in satisfaction than anything else.
She plopped casually back down on the

concrete ledge and waited for Stick Cat to slide the rest of the way to the building.

It took just thirteen seconds for him to make it. He stretched his back paws onto the ledge, released the napkin with his front paws, and lurched toward the building. Stick Cat clung to it with all his remaining strength. The wall was made of bricks and concrete and he dug his front claws into the rough cracks and crevices.

Stick Cat pressed his face and body against the building.

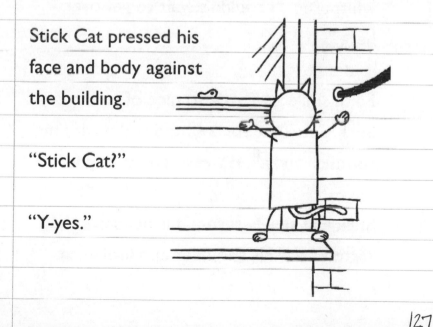

"Stick Cat?"

"Y-yes."

"Why are you hugging the building?"

Stick Cat didn't answer. He tried to catch his breath.

Edith asked another question. There was a hint of mischief in her voice. "Are you *in love* with the building, Stick Cat? Do you want to *marry* it?"

"I'm just happy to be here," Stick Cat whispered. "I couldn't wait to get over here."

Edith smiled. "That's so nice of you to say, Stick Cat. That you wanted to be with me so much and all. It's very sweet of you."

Stick Cat slowly turned his head ever so slightly over his shoulder and looked at

Edith lying on the ledge. About one-third of her body dangled over the edge.

"Let's get inside," he said to Edith.

"Not yet, Stick Cat."

"Why not?"

Edith lifted her chin from the concrete ledge and gazed at Stick Cat. She closed her eyes briefly and then opened them slowly. "Because," she finally explained. "You haven't thanked me yet, that's why."

"Thanked you for what?"

"For helping you slide the rest of the way on the cable, that's what."

Stick Cat turned his head and faced the building again. He really, really, really wanted to get inside. "You mean thank you for jerking that cable so that my entire body flailed around in the air twenty-three floors above the alley?"

"That's right."

"Thank you, Edith," Stick Cat said. "Now let's get inside."

"Not yet."

"Why not?" Stick Cat asked, and glanced back at Edith again.

She stared wide-eyed at him.

"I think you should acknowledge that my

brilliant parachute idea worked to absolute perfection."

"'Absolute perfection'?"

"That's right."

Now, Stick Cat knew the napkin had not worked in the way Edith intended at all. But it was not the time—and this was definitely not the place—to point out this fact. He wanted to get off that ledge. So Stick Cat said simply and quietly, "It was an amazing idea, Edith."

"Thank you," Edith answered, and stood up. "I thought so too."

With that, she hopped through the open window.

And Stick Cat followed her.

Chapter 10

EDITH'S FEMININE
FELINE FIGURE

Stick Cat raced across the large open room
to the huge pot. He passed Edith in the
center of the room. She spun slowly as she
scanned the surrounding area. Stick Cat
heard Edith talk to herself.

"Lox, lox," she
whispered. "Where
would the lox be?"

Stick Cat paid no
attention to Edith and hurried straight to
the ladder. It felt so good to have the solid

floor beneath his paws.

He climbed the ladder quickly. As he did he felt the wet coffee on his paw pads. It was slippery on that smooth metal step and he understood how Hazel had fallen in.

When he reached the top of the ladder, Stick Cat looked down into the pot.

Hazel was shoulder-deep in thick bagel batter. She had splotches of it in her hair and on her arms. Hazel's fingers were wrapped around the rim of the pot.

She stared up at Stick Cat.

"I need help," Hazel said. "I need help, little kitty."

Stick Cat leaned his head down, rubbed his cheek across Hazel's knuckles, and then turned to Edith.

"Over here, Edith!" he called.

Edith was still turning slowly in the middle of the room. She called back, "Did you find some lox over there?"

Stick Cat glanced down at Hazel one more time and then stepped back down the ladder.

"No," he said when he reached the floor. "I found Hazel. She's in the pot. She's stuck. We have to help her!"

"Does she have any lox with her?"

Stick Cat didn't answer Edith's inquiry for several seconds. He dropped his head and stared at the floor. He contemplated his response.

"Well, does she?"

Stick Cat lifted his head and answered, "She doesn't have any lox with her right now," he said. "But if we help her escape from that pot, maybe she'll *reward* us with some lox."

"A reward of lox, hunh?"

"Maybe," Stick Cat suggested.

Edith thought about this idea for almost a full minute. She tilted her head in consideration. When she did, she noticed a shiny, silver refrigerator against the wall and began to use it like a mirror. She licked the back of her left front paw, smoothed her fur, and examined her reflection. She did this three times and was still not satisfied with her appearance.

While Edith groomed herself, Stick Cat looked back and forth between her and Hazel's frail hands clinging to the rim of the pot. Edith began to lick her paw a fourth time when Stick Cat spoke.

"Edith?"

"Yes?" she answered, and turned to him. She didn't appear to appreciate having her grooming interrupted. "What is it now, Stick Cat?"

"The lox reward," Stick Cat said. "Will you help me get Hazel out of the pot? There might be a lox reward."

Edith turned away from him then, checked her reflection, and drew her paw across her brow.

"Lox *are* delicious, right?" Stick Cat added.

This might have been the final bit of urging Edith needed. She turned to Stick Cat and said, "Oh, very well. We're here anyway. But there better be some lox at the end of all this, buster."

"Great!" Stick Cat said quickly. "Now we just have to figure out how to get her out."

"Oh, that's no big deal," Edith said matter-of-factly.

"It's not?"

"No."

"Why?"

"Because I already know how to get her
out, that's why."

"How?!" Stick Cat asked quickly. He was
happy that Edith had a plan. He wanted to
help Hazel as soon as possible.

"It's perfectly obvious," Edith said. She
began to walk toward the ladder. "The pot
is full of bagel batter, right?"

Stick Cat followed after her. "Right."

Edith began to climb
the ladder. At the
second step she
glanced back over her
shoulder and said,
"We eat her way out."

"'Eat her way out'?"

"That's right," confirmed Edith. She reached the top of the ladder and looked down at Hazel. Changing the subject, Edith said, "You're right, Stick Cat. She's not scuba diving, after all."

Stick Cat ignored that comment and instead asked, "What do you mean, 'eat her way out'?"

Edith sat on the top step of the ladder. She put her front paws on her hips and said, "It's food, Stick Cat, food. We jump in and chow down. We keep eating the bagel batter until it gets low enough that Hazel won't be stuck any longer. She can just climb out."

Stick Cat stopped midstride right then, his front left paw suspended in the air. He couldn't believe what he just heard.

"Edith," he said. "It would take us years to eat that much food."

"You think so?"

"I know so."

Edith looked back into the pot. "I'm not so sure about that, Stick Cat," she replied. "I have a pretty healthy appetite. It's truly amazing when I think about it. I mean, how can I eat so much and still maintain my feminine feline figure? It's remarkable really."

"You are remarkable, it's true," Stick Cat said. "Why don't we see if we can come up with a different idea. We'll use the eat-all-the-batter idea as an emergency backup plan."

Edith eyed Stick Cat dubiously.

Stick Cat could see Edith's doubt in her expression and added, "You're so good at coming up with ideas. I'd be shocked if you don't come up with something even better anyway."

"Figure out something that's better than eating all the batter, hmm?" Edith said as much to herself as anyone. "Doesn't seem possible. But if anybody can do it, I can. You're right about that."

Stick Cat began moving again. He sprang to the top step next to Edith and looked down at Hazel once more.

"Hi again, kitty," Hazel sighed. She seemed a little short of breath—as if all that thick, heavy batter was pressing in on her, squeezing the air out of her lungs. "I see you have a friend."

Stick Cat purred at Hazel and rubbed his cheek against her fingers again. He looked into Hazel's eyes. They looked sad and empty. They looked tired and wary.

"I can't hold on much longer," Hazel whispered. "I can barely feel my fingers anymore."

Stick Cat caressed Hazel's hand one additional time and then leaned up close to Edith.

"We don't have much time," he said to her. There was a clear sense of desperation in his voice. Something about the way Hazel looked—and sounded—multiplied Stick Cat's sense of urgency. "There has to be something we can use around here."

Stick Cat hurried down the ladder and scanned the room for possible tools to use. Edith followed him. All he saw were the bags of cloud powder on the shelf next to the sink and hose. The long table had a block of large knives on it. The bagel sign hung over it. There was the large silver refrigerator.

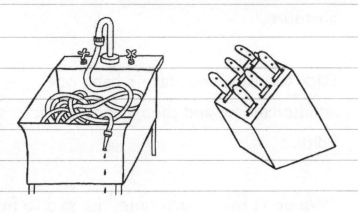

There was nothing else—nothing useful at all.

As Stick Cat continued to look for something he could utilize, Edith offered a series of rapid-fire suggestions.

And Stick Cat offered a series of reasons why her suggestions wouldn't work.

"We could tip the pot over," Edith said.

"I think it must weigh hundreds of pounds."

"Let's build a boat."

"No materials."

"I've got it!" exclaimed
Edith after several
seconds. "We introduce
her to a man. After a few
months, they fall in love.
They want to get married.
He pulls her out to take her to
the church on their wedding day."

"There's no man around."

"How about if we get a fishing pole with a
big hook on the end of the line? We throw it
in the pot, hook Hazel's neck or shoulder or

face or whatever, and pull her out that way."

"Hook her face?"

"Yeah. Whatever."

"No fishing
pole."

Edith turned a squinted, almost angry eye
toward Stick Cat. She was frustrated.

"You don't like any of my plans," Edith said,
and took a menacing step toward Stick Cat.
"You don't take me seriously."

"I love your plans," Stick Cat said quickly,
and tried to explain further. "I'm just not

sure they're very realistic."

Edith huffed.

"Look, Stick Cat," she said. "I think you're forgetting just *who* rescued Mr. Music that one time. It was me who did all the important stuff that day."

"Umm—"

"And what about the parachutes?" Edith went on before Stick Cat could say anything else. "Didn't we float over here using my parachute idea? Didn't we?"

Now, Stick Cat knew they didn't actually "float" across the alley. He knew they slid over. But there was something that Edith had just said that ignited a hint of an idea.

"What did you just say?"

"My parachute plan worked. We floated over here."

"'Floated'?"

"Right. We floated."

Stick Cat whispered, "Floated."

...FLOATED...

And then he snapped his head around that near-empty room. He stared at the hose for a third of a second and then whipped his head around to stare at the bagel sign.

"Floated," he whispered again—this time a little louder.

"Stick Cat," Edith said. Her voice had gone from frustrated and angry to worried instantly. "What's wrong with you?"

Stick Cat turned to Edith then. He looked straight at her.

"Nothing is wrong," he answered. He smiled at her. "You've done it again."

"Done what?"

"You solved the problem. You figured out how we're going to rescue Hazel!"

"I did?" Edith asked. She seemed confused.

"You did! You're a genius!"

Although Edith didn't know what Stick Cat was talking about, she had plenty of confidence in herself as usual. She drew back her shoulders and lifted her chin in the air slightly. Then she said just one thing.

"Tell me something I don't *already* know."

Chapter 11

SNAP! SNAP! THUD!

"We need two things to make your idea work," said Stick Cat.

Edith, you could tell, liked the fact that Stick Cat referred to their rescue strategy as *her* idea. The fact that she didn't know what that idea actually was didn't seem to matter at all. She took ownership of it.

"Of course we do," she said to Stick Cat. Then she asked, "What two things?"

"The hose and the bagel sign," Stick Cat answered as he leaped up to the top step of the ladder again. He wanted to check on Hazel one more time before putting the plan into action.

Hazel didn't look good.

She had sunk a little deeper into the thick, heavy batter. Her shoulders were now under the surface. Her fingers had slid off the pot's rim a bit. Her eyes were squeezed shut, as if she was concentrating very hard—hanging on with whatever strength she had left.

Stick Cat descended the ladder in two

jumps. "The hose and the bagel sign!" he repeated.

"I'll get the sign," Edith said.

Stick Cat nodded and raced toward the hose at the sink.

After he bounded up and into the sink, Stick Cat uncoiled and detangled the hose. He pushed it out over the edge of the sink—and onto the floor.

When he was done, he whipped his head around to check on Edith's progress with the sign.

He both saw her and heard her simultaneously.

"Ya-hoo!" she screamed.

Edith was inside the bagel sign, lying belly-down in its hole.
Her arms were stretched out to her sides like wings. She shifted her weight forward and back to swing higher and higher.

"Edith! What are you doing?!"

She had a thrilled smile on her face.

"I'm getting the sign . . ."

Snap!

Snap!

The two thin strings that suspended the
bagel sign from the ceiling broke loose.

The sign—and Edith—fell to the table with a
THUD!

Her eyes never left Stick Cat. She finished
her sentence.

". . . down."

Stick Cat smiled at her.

"Only a cat of my particular proportion and substantial stature could accomplish such a difficult task," Edith said calmly as she squirmed, squeezed, and squiggled her way out of the center of the sign. "It's really lucky you have me here."

"That's the absolute truth," replied Stick Cat. "Can you get the sign over here by the pot?"

As Edith did that, Stick Cat snatched the end of the hose on the floor and dragged it to the foot of the ladder. He clasped the hose nozzle in his mouth and climbed the rungs on the ladder, pulling steadily and never losing his grip. When he reached the top, Stick Cat hung the hose over the highest step. With it secure there, Stick Cat turned to see how Edith was doing.

She was, to Stick Cat's surprise and pleasure, at the bottom of the ladder sitting on the circular bagel sign.

Edith looked up at him and asked, "Now what do we do to make my plan work?"

He took a quick look at Hazel before answering. She only held on with one hand now. Her other arm was out to her side, atop the thick, dense batter. Her eyes were open. They looked desperate and tired.

"I have to go now, kitty," Hazel whispered.

Stick Cat leaped from the ladder's top step and landed safely on all fours next to Edith and the sign. Edith had never seen Stick Cat jump from such a high place before.

"We have to push this up!" Stick Cat said.

Edith had never heard Stick Cat speak with such urgency.

She hopped off the sign, helped Stick Cat tilt it onto its side, and began to push it up the ladder. With one of them on each side, they could balance the bagel sign and roll it to the top. It bounced awkwardly over each

step, but they maintained its balance and
kept pushing.

Stick Cat eyed the pot's rim when they were
almost to the top. Hazel's hand was no
longer there. Stick Cat pushed harder.

"Don't stop!" he grunted when they reached
the top. "Push it in!"

The sign fell off the ladder, over the pot's

side, and landed in the bagel batter with a
thick, heavy *sp-lunk!*

Edith and Stick Cat leaned over to look into
the pot. The bagel sign
floated atop the batter.

They could only see
Hazel's head now. Her
body was completely
below the surface.

She stared at them as they leaned over.

She glanced sideways at
the bagel sign.

And for the second
time that day, Stick Cat
watched Hazel disappear.

Chapter 12

TWO SMART KITTIES

Hazel was gone.

"No!" Stick Cat yelled.

Edith hung her head.

Stick Cat hung his head.

For three seconds.

And then Hazel rose up through the batter—and up through the hole in the middle of that bagel sign. She pushed her arms through the hole, hooking her elbows securely over the sign.

And she floated.

The gooey batter fell from her face and hair in slow gluey clumps. It took a minute or so for most of it to drip off Hazel's face. She struggled to open her eyes. Her eyelids had batter on them too.

When she got her eyes open, she stared up at Stick Cat and Edith.

A thick clump of batter fell from her chin. Stick Cat could see Hazel's mouth now.

She grinned at him.

"Wow," Edith said next to Stick Cat on top of the ladder. "I had no idea my plan was that good."

"It's not over yet," Stick Cat said. He knew Hazel was relatively safe for the time being. But there was still work to do. She wasn't going to sink now—but Hazel still wasn't out of the pot.

"My plan's not over yet?" Edith asked.

Stick Cat shook his head. He was much more at ease now that Hazel was safer. He looked back into the pot. The desperation had left Hazel's face for now. She floated comfortably in her bagel-sign life-preserver.

"Don't you know the second step of your plan?" Stick Cat asked after turning back to Edith. There was the slightest hint of teasing in his voice.

"Of course I know," Edith responded, and then paused. Then a sly, momentary grin came to her face—as if an idea had suddenly occurred to her. "I just want to see if *you* know."

"Well, I think I do," Stick Cat answered, impressed with her cleverness. "You tell me if I'm right or not."

"Okay."

Stick Cat said, "I'm going to turn the hose on and put it in the pot. As the water fills the pot, Hazel will float higher and higher. When she floats high enough, she'll be able to pull herself out and climb down the ladder."

Edith waited to see if Stick Cat was done. When she was certain he was, she said, "That's my plan exactly, Stick Cat. Way to figure it out!"

"And filling the pot with water provides an extra benefit for Hazel," added Stick Cat.

"It sure does," Edith said slowly. She couldn't quite hide the puzzled look on her face even though she tried. "Let's see if you know what that is too."

Stick Cat nodded and answered, "When we fill the pot with water, the thick bagel batter will be diluted and she'll be able to move around more freely. That will help her climb out of the pot too."

"'Diluted'?" Edith asked. It was clear she didn't know the definition of the word. "*I* know what that word means. But let's see if *you* know what it means."

"It means the batter will get thinner—less

heavy and sticky."

Edith nodded at Stick Cat. "I'm so proud of you," she said. "You really figured out my plan! Wow! How'd you do it?"

"Just a lucky guess, I suppose."

"That makes sense," Edith confirmed. "Just lucky."

Stick Cat hung the hose over the rim of the pot, ensured that it was not aimed at Hazel, and then turned the nozzle. Water began to pour out.

Edith and Stick Cat both peered down into the pot.

"Is it working yet? Is she floating higher?"

"I can't tell," Stick Cat answered. "It's a big pot. It will take a few minutes to see."

While they waited, Hazel talked to them.

"There are the two good kitties," she said. Her voice sounded slightly stronger now. "Two *smart* kitties, I should say."

"I don't know about '*two*,' Edith whispered just loud enough for Stick Cat to hear. "It really was *my* plan."

Hazel looked at the hose as water poured from it. She seemed puzzled by it.

"I don't know what you two are up to now," she said, and sighed. "But I know someone is looking out for me somewhere. I'm not sure you two even exist. Am I dreaming? Am I hallucinating? Am I just imagining you? I don't know."

Hazel closed her eyes and shook her head.

"This bagel sign is real, I know that," Hazel said, and lifted her head to look at them again. "It's like a life preserver in an ocean of bagel batter. You know what? I always liked this sign. It used to hang outside my shop over the sidewalk. Then we got a new sign. I didn't want to just get rid of this old one. Too many memories. That sign hung there for more than thirty years. I hung it up here so I could see it every day—so I could think about all the good things that have happened for me and my shop. We need to take care of the old things, don't you think?"

Stick Cat nodded at her.

Hazel smiled at him. "It's almost like you understand me," she said.

And then Hazel stopped talking altogether. She turned her head left and right quickly. She wriggled her shoulders in the bagel sign.

She looked confused—sort of happily confused—about something. Hazel shifted her head to stare at the water pouring from the hose.

Then she looked up at Stick Cat and Edith.

"I'm floating!"
she exclaimed.
"I understand
now. You two
are so smart!"

Edith whispered, "It was really *my* idea
only."

Stick Cat turned to Edith then.

"We can go now," he said. "She's going to
be okay. We need to get back before Goose
and Tiffany get home."

"What about the lox?!"

"She's not going to be out for a while.
I think we better get back."

"But what about the LOX?!"

"You'll get some Saturday."

"I will?"

"Of course," Stick Cat said. "Today is Friday.
You said Tiffany always gets bagels and lox
on Saturday morning, right?"

"Right," Edith said slowly. She didn't seem
very convinced. "But I don't want to wait
that long."

"It's Friday afternoon right now, Edith,"
Stick Cat said. "Tiffany brings bagels and
lox on Saturday morning. That's not a

very long wait at all."

"It's days and days, Stick Cat!" Edith said, sounding exasperated. "I can't wait that long!"

Stick Cat understood now. Edith didn't know the days of the week—or the order of the days of the week anyway.

"Today is Friday, Edith," Stick Cat explained. "Saturday comes after Friday. Tomorrow is Saturday. Tiffany is bringing lox tomorrow."

"Why didn't you just say that?" Edith asked. She was a little frustrated, but she also seemed to like the idea of getting lox so soon. "Why do you have to make things so complicated?"

"I didn't mean to," Stick Cat said, and glanced away. "Can you wait as long as tomorrow morning?"

Edith stared up at the ceiling for a few seconds. After that pause for consideration, she answered, "I suppose so."

"Great. Then let's—" Stick Cat said.

But he was interrupted by Edith.

"Wait!" she said loudly. "Did you say today is Friday?"

"That's right."

"Excellent!" exclaimed Edith. She slapped her paws together in a muffled clap. "Today is Fonduc Friday! I *love* fondue!"

Stick Cat had no idea what "fondue" was,
but he was happy to see Edith's excitement.
"Good," he said. "Now let's get back."

He dashed to the open window, jumped to
the ledge, and looked across the alley. Edith
leaped up next to him.

Stick Cat saw the problem immediately.

There was no way to get home.

Chapter 13

A FLASH OF RED

It took Stick Cat less than one second to realize what he had done—or, more precisely, what he had failed to notice.

On their original trip across the alley, he and Edith had traveled *down* from the twenty-third floor of their building to the twenty-second floor of Hazel's building.

There was no way to use the same method going back.

They couldn't loop their napkins over the thick black cable and slide *up* to get home.

It wouldn't work.

"What's the matter, Stick Cat?" Edith asked.

"We're stuck," he answered. "Absolutely stuck. We'll never get home."

"Why not?"

"The cable we used to slide—umm, to parachute—our way over here goes up, not down. It's the only cable running between the buildings."

"It doesn't go down anymore?"

"Umm, no."

1ˢᵗ TRIP
DOWN

"It went down before."

2ⁿᵈ TRIP
UP

"I know," Stick Cat said slowly.

"Somebody must have moved it, I guess."

Stick Cat really didn't want to explain anything to Edith right now. He had to figure this out. He had to think of something—fast. So he simply said to Edith, "Yes, I guess somebody moved it."

"We're stuck?" Edith didn't quite seem to believe it.

"Stuck," Stick Cat confirmed.

"Hmm," Edith said, and paused. "Can I ask you a question?"

Stick Cat didn't answer. He scanned the room again—but he already knew what was there. There was a long table, the block with big knives, the sink, the hose. Even the bagel sign was gone. Hazel was still using it as a life preserver. There was absolutely nothing they could use to get across the alley—to get home to Goose and Tiffany.

Edith repeated, "Can I ask you a question?"

"Of course," Stick Cat answered, but he sounded distracted. He looked out the window—left and right, up and down, across the alley.

Nothing.

Left and right he saw the corners of this building. The sky was up. The alley was down—twenty-two floors down. Across the alley, Stick Cat saw his and Edith's building. It seemed so far away now—now that he knew he couldn't reach it. There were window ledges, the fire escape, the black cable—going up.

Nothing else.

Stick Cat sighed. He turned to Edith and said, "What is it that you want to ask me?"

"We're stuck here, right?" Edith asked.

"Right."

"Maybe for the rest of our lives?"

"Maybe," Stick Cat said. A hint of sadness leaked into his voice. "So, what's your question?"

"I was just wondering about something."

"Yes?"

"Where do you think Hazel keeps those lox?"

Stick Cat stared straight into Edith's eyes. She looked completely unconcerned with their predicament. All of her attention was currently focused on finding lox.

"Edith," Stick Cat said. He smiled at her. To him, there was just something funny about her question. "If we are stuck here for the rest of our lives, I can't think of anyone I'd rather be stuck with."

Edith cocked her head in curiosity. She seemed to think very deeply about Stick Cat's words. She closed her eyes slowly and then opened them again just as slowly.

She said, "So, you don't know where the lox might be? Is that what you're saying?"

Stick Cat almost laughed, but he didn't. He loved her perspective, but he didn't laugh—and he didn't speak.

At that precise moment, the bright red cardinal he had seen earlier caught his attention from the corner of his eye.

The flash of red made him turn his head. He stared at that bird as it fluttered down from the garden above and landed in the middle of the thick black cable that stretched between the two buildings. It perched there. It tweeted. The cable swung a bit.

"Do you see that bird?" Edith asked.

"I do," Stick Cat answered, and continued to stare at it.

Edith said, "I sure would like to eat it."

Stick Cat watched the cardinal. It dropped off the cable, fluttered, and flew to the fire escape on his and Edith's building.

Edith watched some more too.

"I'll tell you one thing," she said. "I bet that's one tasty bird."

Stick Cat smiled at the comment. He didn't know why, but Edith was making him feel better about the impossible situation they found themselves in.

The cardinal flew from the fire escape back to the cable. It perched there for seven seconds. Then it glided over to the fire escape.

"Cable to fire escape. Then back," Edith

said, providing play-by-play commentary to the cardinal's movements. "Cable to fire escape. Then back. What a birdbrain."

"What?" Stick Cat asked. "What did you say?"

"'Birdbrain'?"

"No."

"'Cable to fire escape'?"

The cardinal flew up and out of sight—probably to the garden on the roof again, Stick Cat figured.

"Cable to fire escape," he repeated quietly.

Then Stick Cat jerked his head around. He looked at the knife block on the long table. As he leaped off the ledge and back into the room, he called, "I'll be right back!"

Stick Cat made it to the table in three long bounds. He jumped to the tabletop and pulled all the knives from the block. They clattered and clanged onto the table. When they were all out before him, Stick Cat chose the biggest, heaviest, and sharpest knife. He picked it up.

He pushed the knife off the table to the floor and waited for it to settle. Then he jumped to the floor himself. He pushed the knife carefully across the room to the ledge, picked it up, and placed it next to Edith.

After he hopped to the ledge to join Edith, she asked, "What's with the knife? Is it in case the red bird comes back?"

"Umm, no."

"Good. Because I think I can handle that little red gliding bird, no problem," she said with absolute confidence. Then she asked, "What's the knife for then?"

"We're going to use it to get across the alley."

"We are? How?"

Stick Cat thought about his answer for a

moment. He wasn't quite sure what to say to Edith. What he was about to propose would be incredibly dangerous. It had a slim chance of working—but it was their only hope. In the end, he decided the truth was the best way to go.

"We're going to hold on as tight as we can to the cable. I'm going to cut it with this big knife. We'll swing across the alley. When we get really close to our building, we'll let go and land on the fire escape. We'll walk up to your apartment."

Edith said nothing for an entire minute. Stick Cat knew she was probably totally scared by the idea. *He* was totally scared by the idea. Any right-minded cat would be.

Finally, Edith spoke.

"Do you think we should take one more look around for some lox before we go?"

"No," answered Stick Cat as he smiled. "I don't think there's time. We need to get back. So, you like my idea?"

"Well, it's not very clever," Edith said. "It's certainly not as clever as my parachute plan, which worked to absolute perfection."

"I remember," said Stick Cat.

"But it does sound totally fun!" Edith exclaimed. "Let's do it!"

Chapter 14

ALMOST THERE

"Seriously?"

"Sure. Why not?" Edith asked.

"Well, it's a pretty dangerous idea."

Edith shrugged. "Dangerous schm-angerous. Let's do this thing!"

And with that, Edith wrapped herself around the thick black cable. Stick Cat did the same thing with his back legs and picked the heavy knife up with his front legs.

Before he lifted the knife, Stick Cat made sure of two things. He looked over at the bagel batter pot. It was now nearly full. He could see Hazel's hair and forehead. He could see part of her arm and the bagel sign. She was almost out. Then he turned to look at Edith. She was wrapped around the cable, her claws dug into its thick rubber casing. She had an excellent grip.

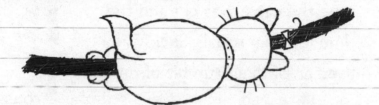

"What are you waiting for?" Edith asked.

And with that, Stick Cat dug his own back claws into the cable.

He raised the knife above his head.

He brought it down as fast and as hard as he could.

He hit the cable perfectly.

SLASH!

There was a half second—or maybe even less—between the time the cable was cut and the time it began to fall. Stick Cat used all of that little bit of time.

He dropped the knife onto the ledge, snatched the now-loose cable with his front claws, closed his eyes—and held on.

The cable fell instantly from the building. They dropped straight down at first and then began to swing toward their own building.

Edith's and Stick Cat's claws dug into the cable's black rubber.

Edith screamed as they fell and swung.

It was not a scream of terror.

It was a scream of delight.

"Wa-hoo!"

Stick Cat opened his eyes.

He had to. Their building approached quickly. Stick Cat didn't look down. He kept his eyes fixed on the fire escape attached to their building.

"Get ready!" he yelled.

"For what?" Edith yelled back.

"To let go!"

"Do we have to?!"

"Yes!"

Stick Cat knew they only had one chance.
If they didn't let go at exactly the right
time—when the downward arc of the cable
was nearest the fire escape—they might
get really hurt crashing into the fire escape
over and over again.

And they couldn't let go too early. If
they did, there was nothing—absolutely
nothing—between them and the alley far
down below.

He watched as they swung closer and closer
to their building.

"Almost there!" he yelled.

The cable lost speed as it reached the end
of its arc. It would start swinging back in the
other direction after it hit the fire escape.
He didn't want to hold on any longer than
he had to.

"Now!" he screamed.

They let go.

Stick Cat and Edith
were suspended in
the air.

Until they landed.

On the fire escape platform.

Edith skidded a bit and then jumped to the edge of the platform. She put her front paws up on the railing.

"Let's go again!" she exclaimed.

Stick Cat pressed against the building's wall as closely as he could. He took comfort in knowing the cable would not be able to swing across again—and he wouldn't need to stop Edith from jumping for it.

The cable smacked against the fire escape, swung back out a little ways and then slapped against it with less and less force a few more times. It quickly settled to stillness.

Edith saw this happen and muttered in genuine disappointment, "Bummer."

She then looked up the fire escape steps to find her apartment. While she looked for the window way up above, Stick Cat looked at the alley way down below.

"How many floors down from my apartment are we?" asked Edith.

"Eight or ten, I think," Stick Cat answered. He had not moved from the wall yet.

"Race you!" Edith yelled, and took off.

Now, fire escape stairs and landings are not like the stairs and landings in our houses and schools.

They're made out of metal—in this case, rusty metal. They're rickety and shaky. The fire escape metal has holes in it so rainwater will drain through it. You can see right through them. They are as much air as they are metal.

None of this mattered to Edith. She leaped and jumped and ran up each set of steps as if it was as simple as jumping up to the kitchen sink. She wanted to win the race.

The fire escape's condition did matter a great deal to Stick Cat, however.

He counted and calculated.

There were ten steps up to each landing. They were about ten floors below Edith's apartment.

"You can do one hundred steps," he whispered to himself. "Don't look down. Just look at the next step. And count. Concentrate on counting."

Edith yelled from above, "I'm going to beat you!"

"One, two," Stick Cat whispered as he started his perilous journey.

After a little while, Edith yelled, "I'm getting closer!"

"Fifteen, sixteen . . ."

There was another period of silence, then, "I can see my window!"

"Thirty-two, thirty-three . . ."

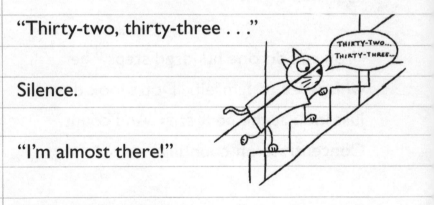

Silence.

"I'm almost there!"

"Forty-eight, forty-nine . . ."

Silence.

"I made it! I win!"

"Sixty-one, sixty-two . . ."

"Stick Cat?"

"Seventy, seventy-one . . ."

"Are you listening to me?"

"Seventy-six, seventy-seven . . ."

"Well, are you?"

"Eighty-three, eighty-four . . ."

"Oh, there you are!"

"Eighty-nine, ninety."

Stick Cat made it. There were nine floors to climb, not ten.

Stick Cat hopped to the ledge next to Edith. He couldn't wait to get inside Edith's apartment—to get on firmer, safer footing. But he didn't go in.

He knew better.

"Edith?" he asked.

"Yes, Stick Cat?"

"Can I come in?"

"How thoughtful of you to ask," she answered graciously. "Please do."

"After you," he said, and waved a paw at the open window.

Then Edith and Stick Cat went in.

Chapter 15

"WHY'S SHE SO WET?"

Edith asked Stick Cat, "What took you so long?"

He'd been inside Edith's apartment a couple of minutes. Stick Cat's heart was just now slowing its pace. He started to breathe normally too.

He answered, "I was just, umm, enjoying the view."

"Oh, good idea," Edith said. "I hung my head

over the edge twice. It made me so dizzy! Did you do that?"

"I felt dizzy, yes."

"It's fun, isn't it?"

"That's one word for it," Stick Cat answered quietly.

Edith was distracted by something out the window. She rose up on her back paws and placed her front paws on the windowsill.

"Hey, look!" she exclaimed. "It's Hazel."

Stick Cat hurried over to the window and stretched to see out as well. He was confident Hazel had made it out of the pot. She had nearly floated to the top before

they swung across the alley. Still, Stick Cat
wanted to make sure.

"Why's she so wet?" asked Edith.

Stick Cat turned to see if Edith was joking.

She wasn't.

"She was in the bagel pot, remember?"

"Oh, right," Edith said. "She went for a
swim. I forgot."

"She fell into the pot, Edith," Stick Cat said.
"That's why we had to rescue her."

"I *know* we had to rescue her," Edith said. "But I still think she could have been swimming. Look at that inner tube lying by the pot. People always take inner tubes when they go swimming."

Stick Cat stared at Edith with great intensity.

She still wasn't kidding.

"That's the bagel sign, Edith," he said.

"Hmm," she said. "People will use anything for inner tubes, I guess."

Stick Cat decided to look at Hazel instead of Edith. He thought it would be less confusing.

Hazel stood at the window on the twenty-second floor of the building across the alley. Her clothes hung heavily on her—soaked with bagel batter and  water. Her gray hair was matted against her head. She looked tired and uncomfortable.

And she also looked relieved— happy even. For a moment—a brief second only—she seemed to stare at Edith and him. She was too far away for Stick Cat to tell for sure.

"What's she doing now?" asked Edith.

Hazel pointed at the corner of their building and shifted her finger in little jerks toward Edith's apartment. Then she made the same kind of movement from the roof down to Edith's apartment.

"I have no idea," answered Stick Cat after a moment of observation. "It looks like she's counting or something."

Edith didn't respond.

There was a good reason for that.

She was asleep right there on the floor beneath the window. Stick Cat had not even seen her drop down.

He hopped up to the window, closed it, and then came back down to the floor.

He looked at Edith.

She looked perfectly at peace. Seeing her so comfortable and still made Stick Cat feel suddenly sleepy too.

It had been a long, scary, invigorating day. He thought about going home through their hole to his apartment, but tiredness swept over him like a warm breeze.

Stick Cat settled down next to Edith.

He fell quickly—and deeply—asleep.

Chapter 16

LOX

"Stick Cat!"

It was Edith.

"Someone's at the door!" she said in an emphatic whisper. "It must be Tiffany!"

Stick Cat was up and on his feet instantaneously. It took him just a few seconds to get his bearings. They had been asleep for some time. He could tell it was late in the day—the fading brightness outside told him that. Goose would get home soon too.

"Okay!" Stick Cat said. He hustled to the bathroom and Edith followed him. She would need to close the cabinet door behind him once he got through the hole.

They got there fast and Stick Cat climbed into the cabinet.

"See you Monday," Stick Cat said.

But Edith didn't answer. She turned her head around to look back through the bathroom door out to the living room.

"Wait here a sec," Edith said.

She left the bathroom and was gone for less than a minute.

"It wasn't Tiffany," Edith said to Stick Cat when she got back. "It must have been a neighbor or something."

"Oh," said Stick Cat.

"You can stay a little longer if you'd like."

Stick Cat smiled at the invitation. "I'd like to," he answered. "But it's been a busy day. And Goose and Tiffany will be home soon anyway."

Right then they both
heard keys jingle and
the lock turn to Edith's
apartment door.

"*That's* her," Stick Cat
said.

"Will you stay here while I go make sure?"
Edith asked.

Stick Cat nodded. He climbed through the
hole—and then waited for Edith to return.
He was certain it was Tiffany. And he knew
Edith would come and close the cabinet
door. That was something they both always
remembered to do. Then Tiffany spoke—
and it made him stop and turn his head.

"Look what was outside our door," Tiffany said. Stick Cat could hear her talk to Edith in the living room. "A big bag from Hazel's Bagels. I have no idea what it's doing here. There are bagels and cream cheese. Even lox!"

Stick Cat heard Edith purr loudly then.

"Oh, I see," said Tiffany. "You want to be petted now that I have lox, hunh?"

Stick Cat smiled at that comment.

"I'll put some lox on this napkin just as a special treat for a special kitty."

Stick Cat heard Edith purr loudly again.

"I'm going to go make some tea," Tiffany said. Stick Cat heard Tiffany's footsteps move across the living-room carpet and reach the kitchen, where there was a tile floor.

Everything was fine now. He climbed out of his bathroom cabinet and began to shut the door.

But he stopped before it was shut.

"Pssst!"

It was Edith.

He opened the door fully and saw Edith through the hole. Something hung from her mouth. It was pinkish.

"What's that?" he whispered.

"It's lox!" Edith mumbled without dropping
it. "Here."

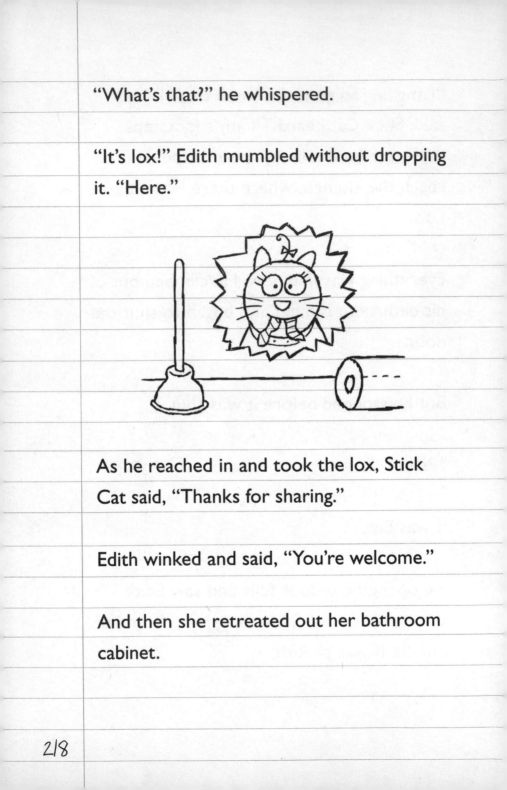

As he reached in and took the lox, Stick
Cat said, "Thanks for sharing."

Edith winked and said, "You're welcome."

And then she retreated out her bathroom
cabinet.

Stick Cat smiled and exited his side.

He put the lox down on the bathroom floor.
He sniffed them. He licked them.

He smiled.

He was right about Hazel—she *did* reward
them with lox.

And Edith was right
about lox.

Lox were delicious.

THE END

Tom Watson is the author of the Stick Dog series. There are currently six books in that series—and more to come.

He lives in Chicago with his wife, daughter, and son. He also has a dog, as you could probably guess. The dog is a Labrador-Newfoundland mix. Tom says he looks like a Labrador with a bad perm. He wanted to name the dog "Put Your Shirt On" (please don't ask why), but he was outvoted by his family. The dog's name is Shadow. Shadow gives Tom lots of ideas for the Stick Dog series.

Tom Watson is also the author of the new Stick Cat series.

Tom does not have a cat. So his ideas for the Stick Cat series come from a whole different place. He's not sure where that place is exactly, but he knows it's kind of strange there.

Visit him online at stickdogbooks.com!

Also available as an ebook.